CARL CAUGHT A
FLYING FISH

CARL CAUGHT A

FLYING FISH

KEVIN O'MALLEY

Simon & Schuster
Books for Young Readers

SIMON & SCHUSTER BOOKS FOR YOUNG READERS
An imprint of Simon & Schuster Children's Publishing Division
1230 Avenue of the Americas
New York, New York 10020

Designed by Heather Wood
The text of this book is set in Berliner Grotesk Light.
The illustrations were created using a thermographic technique and
colored pencils, markers, and gesso on colored Pantone paper.
Manufactured in the United States of America
First Edition
2 4 6 8 10 9 7 5 3 1

Library of Congress Cataloging-in-Publication Data
O'Malley, Kevin, 1961–
Carl caught a flying fish / by Kevin O'Malley
p.   cm.
Summary: Because the flying fish which he caught gives him nothing but trouble
both at home and at school, Carl throws it back into the water.
ISBN 0-689-80098-3
[1. Flying fishes–Fiction. 2. Fishes–Fiction. 3. Stories in rhyme.] I. Title.
PZ8.3.052Car 1996 [E]–dc20 95-1756 CIP AC

For Connor

Carl caught a flying fish,
Flying fish,
Flying fish.
Carl caught a flying fish
Who grinned and said, "Let's roam!"

They played together all day long,
All day long,
All day long.
They played together all day long,
Then Carl took him home.

He gave the fish a place to swim,
Place to swim,
Place to swim.
He gave the fish a place to swim,
But it just wasn't right.

The fish ate everything in sight,
Thing in sight,
Thing in sight.
The fish ate everything in sight,
And didn't share a bite.

He took up all the room in bed,
Room in bed,
Room in bed.
He took up all the room in bed
And had an awful smell.

He followed Carl
      to school next day,
School next day,
School next day.
He followed Carl
      to school next day . . .

To be his show-and-tell.

He made the teacher
 yell and shout,
Yell and shout,
Yell and shout.
He made the teacher
 yell and shout . . .

Then tied him up with rope.

Things were getting
        out of hand,
Out of hand,
Out of hand.
Things were getting
        out of hand
And there was just
        no hope.

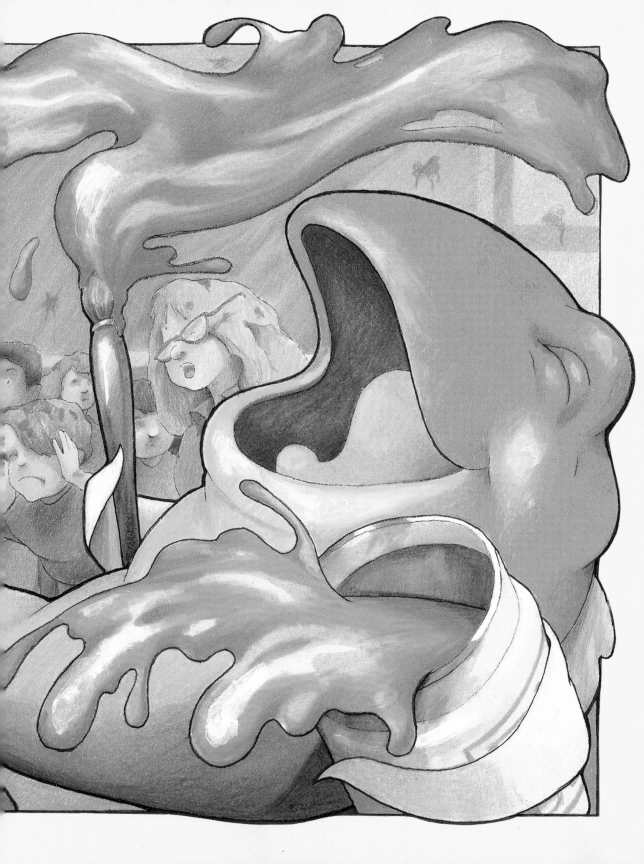

So Carl grabbed his fishing rod,
Fishing rod,
Fishing rod.
He grabbed his trusty fishing rod
And nabbed that naughty fish.

The fish cleaned up the mess he made,
Mess he made,
Mess he made.
The fish cleaned up the mess he made,
And tried to make amends.

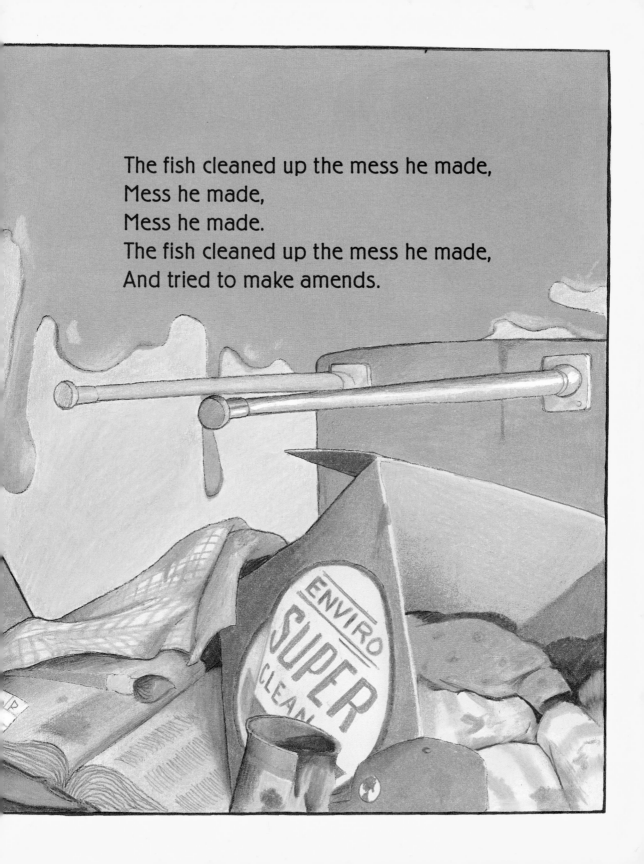

But Carl took him down the road,
Down the road,
Down the road.
Carl took him down the road—
He knew who had to win.

If you ever catch a flying fish,
Flying fish,
Flying fish,
If you ever catch a flying fish,
Just throw him right back in!